Enid Blyton's
NODDY

Purnell

Originally published as six titles:
Noddy goes to the Fair
Noddy and his Passengers
Noddy gives a Tea Party
Noddy and the Noah's Ark Adventure
Noddy and the Runaway Wheel
Noddy's Aeroplane

in 1967, 1970, 1971, 1972, 1977

First published in a single volume 1989

Macdonald & Co (Publishers) Ltd
66-73 Shoe Lane
London EC4P 4AB

a member of Maxwell Pergamon Publishing Corporation plc

ISBN 0-361-08596-6
Printed in DDR
by Sachsendruck Plauen

Contents

Noddy goes to the Fair.................................... 5

Noddy and his Passengers............................. 25

Noddy gives a Tea Party................................ 45

Noddy and the Noah's Ark Adventure.......... 67

Noddy and the Runaway Wheel..................... 87

Noddy's Aeroplane.. 109

NODDY
GOES TO THE FAIR

Hallo, little Noddy! See, here he comes out of his garage with his little car.

"Parp-parp!" That's the hooter telling everyone that Noddy is coming. Does anyone want to hire his car to take them anywhere?

Noddy is a good driver, and if you want to go to the station he will take you there safely.

Here he comes. Look out, Mr. Milkman. Have you left Noddy's bottle of milk for him this morning? And here is the postman, too, with a bundle of letters for little Noddy.

"Hey!" he calls. "Stop a minute, Noddy. I've some letters for you!"

"Put them into my letter-box!" shouts Noddy. "I can't stop for them now."

Mr. and Mrs. Tubby Bear wave goodbye to him.

"Have a good day, with lots of passengers," Mrs. Tubby calls.

"Goodbye!" calls Noddy. "I'll be back tonight with a lot of money in my pocket. I'll be sure to come in and see you!"

Noddy went along the road, humming a little

song. "I'm happy today, hip-hip-hurray. I'm merry and gay, and happy today!"

He kept a good look-out for passengers, but he didn't see anyone for a long time. Dear, dear, did no one want a trip in his little car today?

Ah—there's Monkey, and he's waving to Noddy. "Hey, Noddy, stop! I want to go to the shops and buy a birthday present for my Aunt Big-Eyes."

Noddy stops. "Get in," he says. "What shop do you want to go to?"

"To the sweet-shop," says Monkey. "My Aunt Big-Eyes likes chocolates. I'll buy her a big box."

"You like chocolates too, don't you, Monkey?" says Noddy, driving off. "Aha! You're buying your aunt chocolates so that you can share her present with her! I know your little ways, Monkey!"

"Here's the sweet-shop," says Monkey, jumping out. "Ooooh—what a big box of chocolates I can see. I wonder if I've enough money to buy that?"

"Well, you pay me my fare before you go shopping!" says Noddy, pulling Monkey back by the sleeve. "You owe me two pence!"

And Monkey had to pay him before he went into that sweet-shop!

Noddy drove slowly along the road after Monkey had got out. "I really must find another passenger," he thought. "I've only had one this morning."

"Hey, Noddy! Hey, Noddy! Can't you see me waving to you?" called a loud voice—and there was Mr. Teddy standing at the edge of the pavement, waving his big top hat at Noddy.

Noddy stopped his little car just by him, and Mr. Teddy got in.

"I want to go to the Toy Farm," he said, "and get some eggs for my breakfast. Then I want you to take me to the station, Noddy. I must catch a train."

"Goodness—we'll have to be very quick then!" said Noddy, and drove off to the farm.

The farmer gave Mr. Teddy a dozen new-laid eggs for his breakfast. Then Mr. Teddy said, "Now drive to the station, Noddy, as quickly as you can."

Well, Noddy turned his car round to leave the farm, and dear me, what did he do but run backwards into the pond! What a to-do there was!

"For goodness' sake, Noddy, drive to the station! Look at my watch—we've got four minutes. I shall miss my train!" said Mr. Teddy.

So Noddy went off at top-speed, making all the farmer's hens scuttle away in fright.

"I shall miss my train, I shall miss my train," Mr. Teddy kept saying.

"Oh do be quiet," said Noddy. "I can't drive any faster. I nearly knocked that lamp-post down."

"I can hear the engine whistle," said Mr. Teddy. "I shall miss my train."

But no, here they are at the station and the train is

still there. Mr. Teddy leapt out of the car and hurried to catch the train.

Good—he has caught his train after all!

Then Noddy sees Jumbo hailing him. "Hey, Noddy, take me home, will you? I've been walking for miles and my feet won't walk any more!"

"Get in, Jumbo," says Noddy, and in he got, making the little car lean on one side with his weight!

Off they go. Jumbo is so very big that poor Noddy is quite squashed.

Then Jumbo hears some music. "Oh look, Noddy!" he says. "It's a fair. Shall we go and see it?"

"Oooh yes," says Noddy. "I do like fairs. There is a roundabout, Jumbo."

What a lovely fair! "Let's go on the roundabout, do let's!" cries Noddy.

And there are swings and hoop-las and lucky dips.

"I want to go on the roundabout! I want to go on the swings!" shouts Noddy. "I want to knock down a coconut!"

"Well, as you drove me very well in your car, I will pay for you," says big Jumbo, and he puts his long trunk into his pocket and pulls out his purse.

What a lovely time Noddy is having at the fair! First he had a ride on the roundabout, and he chose a

horse to sit on, one that went up and down as well as round and round. Goodness, what a horse!

Jumbo was funny. He rode on an elephant!

Then they went on some flying swings that went round and round and flew out into the air as they went. Noddy's hat fell off when he was on the swings, and he nearly fell off himself, trying to catch it.

The roundabout man picked it up and gave it to Noddy when he got off his swing. "You'd better pin it on!" he said.

"I'd like to go up in a balloon!" said Jumbo.

"Well, there's one up there," said Noddy, pointing. "It's coming down, Jumbo, do let's go and see it."

Well, the balloon came down and down, and Noddy saw that there was a doll in it, with a monkey.

"Hey!" cried Noddy. "My friend wants to have a trip. Come down to the ground and let him get in."

"He's too big to get in," said the doll, with a giggle.

"But we can lasso him with a rope!" cried the monkey.

And would you believe it, the monkey undid a rope with a big loop at its end and let it down out of the balloon basket.

Jumbo is caught by the end of the rope. You had better hold on very tight, Jumbo!

Big-Ears has come to say that Noddy's car is gone —he saw someone take it!

"I was riding by on my bicycle, looking for you, Noddy," he says, "and I suddenly saw someone jump into your car and drive it away!"

"Oh, my car, my dear little car!" wails Noddy.

"Look!" cries Big-Ears, "the thief has got your car on the ferry-boat. But don't worry, we'll go after him. I'll get a speed-boat, quick!"

Big-Ears got a fine speed-boat, and he and Noddy climbed in. Then they saw Mr. Plod the policeman on the jetty.

"Mr. Plod! We're after a car-thief!" cries Big-Ears. "Jump in!"

And here they all three go after that ferry-boat. Quick, Big-Ears, quick, Noddy, catch the ferry and get the thief!

R-r-r-r-r-r goes the speed-boat—it's going at top speed.

Well, the speed-boat soon caught up the ferry-boat. How frightened the thief was when he saw Mr. Plod the policeman!

"Stop!" cried Mr. Plod, in his sternest voice. "Stop, I say! How dare you steal Noddy's car!"

The ferry-boat stopped. Mr. Plod and Noddy climbed on board. Mr. Plod took hold of the thief at once and held him tightly.

"Can I have my car and get Big-Ears to help me

to put it into the speed-boat?" said Noddy. "I think we can manage."

And somehow they got Noddy's little car into the speed-boat. R-r-r-r-r-r, off they go over the water back to the jetty, where everyone is waiting to cheer them.

"Mr. Plod's taking the thief to the police-station on the other side of the harbour!" shouts Noddy. "And I've got my car back safely, look!"

"Hurrah!" shouts everyone. "Hip-hip-hurrah!"

A Sailor Doll helped Noddy to get the car out of the speedboat, and Big-Ears gave a big push too. At last it was safely on the jetty. Now Noddy can drive again.

"Come home with me, Noddy," said Big-Ears. "We need a rest after all this excitement!"

"Put your bicycle on the back of my car and we'll go to your little toadstool house," said Noddy. "I don't really feel as if I want to pick up any more passengers today."

So off they went in Noddy's car, with Big-Ears' bicycle tied behind. And soon they came to Big-Ears' toadstool house.

Who are these people looking in at the window?

Why, it's Mr. and Mrs. Tubby Bear. Big-Ears had invited them to tea that day, and here they are, wondering why there is no one to open the door to them!

"The house is empty!" says Mr. Tubby.

"Where can Big-Ears be?" says Mrs. Tubby.

"Here he is, with little Noddy!" says Mr. Tubby.

"Big-Ears, have you forgotten that you asked us to tea today?" cries Mrs. Tubby.

Well, would you believe it, Big-Ears had quite forgotten, he had been so upset and excited when Noddy's car was stolen!

"Oh, I'm so sorry!" he said. "Mrs. Tubby, I quite forgot that I'd asked you both to tea—and I've forgotten to buy any cakes or buns or ice-cream! Do forgive me!"

"He forgot about it because he had to chase a ferry-boat to get back my car, which was stolen," said

Noddy, and that made Mr. and Mrs. Tubby feel quite excited. They had to hear the whole story, of course!

"Now listen, you and Noddy must come back to tea with us!" said kind Mrs. Tubby. "I've plenty of cakes, and we can buy some ice-cream on the way."

Wasn't that nice of them? Noddy and Big-Ears were glad to think they wouldn't have to sit on Big-Ears' couch, looking at a table with nothing on it to eat!

The tea-party is in Mrs. Tubby Bear's garden, and what a lovely lot of things there are to eat! There is tea to drink, and orangeade and lemonade too.

Mr. Jumbo has been asked as well, and here he comes to join in, longing to hear all about the story of the stolen car.

"I've got a story to tell you, too!" he says, sitting

down very carefully. "The balloon took me high up in the air—and then the rope broke!"

"Oh dear—did you fall down?" asks Noddy.

"Well, I certainly didn't fall up!" says Mr. Jumbo. "I came down with such a bump that I'm bruised all over. That is why I sat down so very very carefully."

"Have an ice-cream, poor Jumbo!" says Mrs. Tubby Bear. "Have a bun! Have a piece of chocolate-cake. Help yourself to everything, poor Mr. Jumbo."

What a wonderful tea-party they had—wouldn't you like to be there too?

NODDY

AND

HIS PASSENGERS

One day Noddy went to see his friend Big-Ears who lives in this dear little toadstool house up in the woods. And now he is knocking on the door.

"Come in," said Big-Ears. "I'm just going to have a cup of cocoa and a chocolate biscuit. You can share them with me, Noddy." So here they are sitting at Big-Ears' table.

And then someone knocked at the door again. "Is Little Noddy here? I want to go to the station, please." It is Mrs. Bunny with two small bunnies. Look at them!

Noddy took Mrs. Bunny and the two little ones to the station, and Mrs. Bunny paid him ten pence—five pence for herself and half-price for the two small bunnies.

Then Noddy saw them off in the Toyland train. What a crowd there was at the station! There was Mr. Tubby Bear, look—and Mrs. Tubby to see him off.

And there was Mr. Wobbly-Man wobbling about all over the place. Noddy had to give him a push into a carriage because Mr. Wobbly-Man had no legs. He just wobbled everywhere.

The Toyland train went off, chuff-chuff-chuffing, and all its carriages were full. There it goes, off to Humming-Top Town, and Rocking-Horse Village, and Clockwork-Clown Town. What fun!

Noddy waved till it was out of sight, then he went to find some more passengers to take about in his car. Parp-parp! Who wants him today? Somebody is sure to.

Ah—who is that waving to him? It is a clockwork clown. "Hey, Noddy! I want to go to my Uncle Click's. Can you take me?" And into the little car he jumps.

"I'm a bit late," said the clown. "Will you go quickly, please, Noddy?" So here they go at top speed, bumpity-bump. Goodness! Be careful, Noddy! BE CAREFUL!

Noddy and the clown went along quickly in the car, and then there came an extra big bump. The clown nearly shot out of his seat—and, look, what's that flying out of his back?

It's his key! The key that winds him up. Oh dear—there it lies on the road! Neither the clown nor Noddy knows that it is there. Stop, Noddy, stop!

"I want winding up," said the clown. "Noddy, be
a dear and wind me, will you? My key's at the back
of me." "It isn't," said Noddy, looking hard. "Oh—
where can it be?"

The clown was very upset because he had lost his key. "It must have jumped out of me in one of those bumps," he said. "You shouldn't have driven so fast."

"But you *told* me to," said Noddy. "Get into the car again and we'll go back and look for the key." But the clown couldn't move until he was wound up again!

So Noddy went off alone in the car to look for the key. He remembered the place where the car had had a big BUMP and he stopped there and got out. But there was no key.

Noddy called to a teddy-bear who was sweeping the road. "Have you seen a key anywhere?" The teddy-bear nodded. "Yes—Miss Fluffy Cat picked it up and went off with it."

"Bother!" said Noddy. "Now I must go and ask her for it."
So off he goes to Miss Fluffy's house. "Please give me that key
you found," said Noddy.

"Oh dear—I thought it belonged to the clockwork mouse,"
said Miss Fluffy Cat. "I took it to him, but he was out—so I left
it with his mother. I'm so sorry."

"Now I've got to go to the clockwork mouse's,"
said Noddy, quite cross. Off he goes—and now he
is asking the little clockwork mouse. "Where is
it?" he says.

"Oh dear—when I found it wasn't mine I took it over to the clockwork car," said the mouse. "It winds up with a key, you know, and I thought the little driver had lost it."

"Bother this key!" said Noddy, and got into his car to go to get the lost key from the man who drove the clockwork car. But *he* hadn't got it either!

"It wasn't mine after all," said the clockwork-car man. "So I took it to the clock-shop and gave it to Mr. Dong. I thought he might know whose it was."

"Bother, bother, bother!" said Noddy, and drove off to the clock-shop. He went inside. Goodness, what a noise of ticking and tocking! Look at all the dozens of clocks.

Mr. Dong wasn't there. He had gone out. So Noddy spoke to Mrs. Dong about the key. "Oh, Mr. Dong has it," she said. "He took it with him, I don't know why!"

Noddy was just asking Mrs. Dong where Mr. Dong was, when all the clocks in the shop began to strike eleven o'clock. Goodness, what a noise they made — dong, ding, ding, dong!

One big grandfather clock donged so loudly just by Noddy that he was scared and ran out of the shop. He jumped into his car and drove off at top speed.

"I'll have to go and tell the clockwork clown I *can't* find his key," said Noddy. "I suppose he'll still be waiting." But no— he wasn't where Noddy had left him. He shouted loudly.

Well, after Noddy had shouted for the clown he had a great surprise. Look—here he is, walking right out of his uncle's house —he's not standing still any more!

"Hallo!" he said. "Where have you been all this
time? Look—I've got my key again!" Noddy stared
at it. "Well, to think I've been to *heaps* of people
about it!" he said.

"Mr. Dong brought it to me," said the clown. "He said the clockwork-car man took it to him, and he guessed it belonged to me. He's just having lunch with me."

"What a waste of my morning!" said Noddy. But it wasn't—because the clown made him come in and have lunch with his Uncle Click and Mr. Dong—and it *was* a nice one!

NODDY
GIVES A TEA PARTY

NODDY was giving a tea-party for all his friends.

He wrote six letters inviting them to tea, and gave them to the postman to take to his friends.

Noddy was watching for the postman the next morning, and when he came through the gate, Noddy could see some letters in his hand.

"SIX letters for you this morning, Noddy," said the post-man.

Noddy opened the letters, and all his friends said they would love to come to his tea-party.

Noddy put the letters behind the clock on the mantel-piece, and started to get ready. He was going to be very, very busy.

First of all he cleaned his house from top to bottom. He

polished and scrubbed and dusted, until he could see his face in everything. It was as clean as a new pin.

"Now I must bake a cake," said Noddy.

So Noddy baked a big cake and some little cakes. He cut some very thin bread and butter, and made some sand-wiches, and then he put it all on the table. It did look nice.

Noddy sat down in his chair and looked at it. He was very pleased, because he was all ready for the tea-party.

Noddy sat in his chair and looked round the room, and then he began to frown, because Noddy only has one chair, you know. So where were all his friends going to sit? He couldn't ask them to sit on the floor, could he?

"Oh dear," said Noddy. "Whatever shall I do?"

"Milko! Milko!"

Noddy heard the clink of milk bottles, and the Milkman put his head round the door.

"How many bottles to-day Noddy?" he asked.

"Three bottles please, Mr. Milkman," said Noddy sadly.

The Milkman put the bottles down and stared at Noddy, because he was crying.

Plop! Plop!

Two big tears fell on the floor.

"Why are you crying, Noddy?" asked the Milkman.

So Noddy told him all about his tea-party and the chairs.

The Milkman took off his hat and scratched his head, and he thought very hard indeed.

"You'll have to ask them all to bring a chair with them," he said.

Noddy thought that was a very good idea.

He got out his little car, and drove all the way to Big Ears' house.

Knock! Knock!

"Hallo, Noddy," said Big Ears when he opened the door. "I was just coming to your tea-party."

Noddy told his friend about the chairs, and Big Ears' eyes grew round.

"I can't carry my chair all that way, Noddy," he said. "It's too heavy."

Noddy looked at the big arm chair in Big Ears' house, and he knew Big Ears was right. It was much too heavy.

But Big Ears had a better idea. He pulled his chair out into the road, and tied it to the back of Noddy's car.

"Off you go, Noddy," he shouted, as he climbed in beside his friend.

Noddy drove very slowly along the road. The chair had big
castors on it, so it ran along quite easily. They stopped outside
Pink Cat's house, and tied her chair behind Big Ears' chair.
And then Noddy drove down the road to Mr. Plod's house.

Mr. Plod the Policeman frowned just a tiny bit when he saw the chairs trailing behind Noddy's car, but he went and fetched his own without a word, when Noddy told him he couldn't go to the tea-party without it.

So they tied Mr. Plod's chair on behind the others, and then they fetched a very posh gold chair from Angela Golden-hair's house. And last of all they stopped outside Sailor Doll's house, and tied on a simply lovely old rocking chair.

Noddy drove his little car all the way through Toy Village, with the chairs bumping and swaying behind him, and then he stopped outside his own house.

"Goodness, Noddy," said Mrs. Tubby Bear when she saw all the chairs. "What *are* you doing?"

Noddy told her about the chairs, and then he and Big Ears carried them all into his house. They very nearly filled the room, and when Mrs. Tubby staggered round with her best armchair, they only just managed to squeeze it inside.

One by one all Noddy's friends knocked on his door, came inside and sat down on their chairs, until they were all there.

And then Noddy cut the cake and the tea-party began. Everybody said that Noddy's cake was the nicest one they had ever tasted. So Noddy was very happy. His head began to nod. Nid-Nod! And he sang a little song.

Tap my head,
And it goes nid-nod!
Tap it again.
Oh! isn't it odd?
I'm a nodding man
As you can tell,
With a nid-nod head
And a jingle bell.
Wiggle my hat,
And jingle it goes.
It jingles and jangles,
So tap with your toes.
I've a nid-nod head
And a jingle bell hat,
And Noddy's my name,
So that is that.

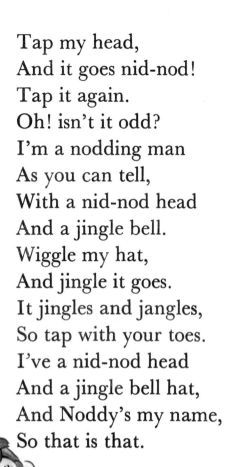

It *was* a lovely tea-party, wasn't it?

NODDY

AND THE

NOAH'S ARK ADVENTURE

One day Mr. Noah came knocking at little Noddy's
front door. "Hey, Noddy!" he said. "Do you know
what we are going to do?"

"No, what?" asked Noddy, opening his door.

"We're going to sail away across the bay for a
lovely little trip!" said Mr. Noah.

"It's a long time since my Ark had a trip across the water. Do come and see us off!"

Noddy got into his little car, and Mr. Noah jumped in beside him. Off they went to the Ark.

Dear me, how grand it looked bobbing up and down on the water! It had been on dry land for a long time—and now Mr. Noah had had it pulled to the water-side.

The Ark animals were very excited. "Come with us, Noddy!" they cried. "Do come!"

"No, I've got too much work to do, taking people about in my little car," said Noddy. "I'll wave goodbye to you and then I'll look out every day for you to come back. Don't be too long, will you?"

The animals looked out of the Ark and waved to Noddy. Mr. Noah ran up the wooden passage-way to the Ark and called to him. "Undo the mooring-rope, Noddy—we're off!"

So Noddy undid the rope that was round the little stone post—and then the great Ark moved slowly away from the jetty.

"We're off, we're off!" cried Mrs. Noah. The lions roared, the elephants trumpeted, the bears grunted—dear me, what a noise and excitement there was.

"There they go!" said Noddy. "Goodbye—and DO come back soon!"

He watched the Noah's Ark sail away across the sea. It got smaller, and at last Noddy could only just see it, a little speck far, far away. He did hope they would all be safe.

It seemed very strange without the Ark and all the animals in Toyland Village. A whole week went by and nothing was heard of them at all.

Noddy was worried. So was Big-Ears. They went to see Mr. Plod the policeman about it.

"Do you think something has happened to the Ark?" said Noddy. "Last night a very big wind blew."

"And there was thunder and lightning," said Big-Ears. "The waves were very big, Mr. Plod. You don't think the Ark has been ship-wrecked, do you?"

"Dear me—what a dreadful thought!" said Mr. Plod. "I think we ought to do something about this.

"I know! I will send out two sailor dolls in a boat, and tell them to ask the little mermaids in the water if they have heard anything about the Ark."

"A very good idea," said Big-Ears.

"And perhaps Captain Heave-Ho could take a toy steamer and cruise round a little to see if he can see any sign of the Ark," said Mr. Plod.

"Yes. And we might get the teddy bears to row about in their little boats round the cliffs to see if *they* can see the Ark," said Big-Ears.

"And I've got an idea too," said Noddy. "We could get Dilly Doll to go up in the toy balloon and sail right over the sea and look down on the water for the Ark. I'm sure one of the sailor dolls would go with her."

"That's a *very* good idea!" said Mr. Plod. "I'll go and see about all these things at once."

Mr. Plod met Dilly Doll and he asked her about her balloon, and told her what he wanted her to do.

"Oh, I'll certainly go up if somebody will go with me," said Dilly Doll. "It would be easy to see the dear old Ark from a balloon high up in the air."

"Take one of the sailor dolls with you," said Mr. Plod.

So Dilly Doll and a sailor were soon high up in the air, bobbing in the wind, trying to see where the Ark had got to.

Then Mr. Plod sent the little teddy bears out in their boats round the cliffs. "You must see if the Ark has got thrown on to some rocks," he said. "Away you go!"

And away they went, bobbing about in their tiny boats, looking for the Ark.

Mr. Plod found Captain Heave-Ho just about to chug away in his toy steamer. "You might go out as far as you can and have a look for the Ark," said Mr. Plod. "It ought to be home again by now."

"Aye-aye," said little Captain Heave-Ho, and away over the water he chugged in his little steamer.

Then the little bears bobbed in to shore in their boats. "We saw some mermaids and they said that Mr. Noah had lost his way."

The next day back came the two sailors in their little boat. "Hey, Noddy! Hey, Big-Ears!" they called. "We didn't see the Ark—but *we* saw some little mermaids too."

"What news did they tell you?" asked Noddy.

"They said that Mr. Noah got muddled between East and West and South and North," said the sailors. "So he sailed home the wrong way, and he's miles and miles away!"

"Here's Captain Heave-Ho coming back," said Big-Ears. "What's *your* news, Captain?"

"I saw the Ark!" called the Captain. "But it was sailing the wrong way so fast that I couldn't catch it up."

"Well, well—we'll just have to hope that the toy balloon will catch it and help it somehow," said Big-Ears.

And will you believe it, the balloon really did catch up the Ark! Mr. Noah suddenly saw it sailing overhead and heard the sailor calling. "You're going the wrong way! Hey, catch this rope and tie it round one of your chimneys! The wind is changing and we can guide you the right way home."

And that very afternoon, when Noddy and Big-Ears went down to the jetty to look again for the Ark, what a shout they gave!

"Here it comes, look! Here it is! It's tied to a balloon-rope—what a very clever idea!"

Everyone came running down to the jetty to watch the great Ark bobbing slowly in. How they cheered!

Bump! The Ark was just beside the jetty.

Mr. Noah put down the gangway, and the animals began to crowd down it, glad to get on shore again.

"Have an ice-cream!" said Big-Ears, ringing his bell loudly. "Come along, Mrs. Noah—you have one too. The ice-cream man is here, and there are lots of people to give you a grand welcome home again!"

Big-Ears roped the Ark to the mooring-post. "There!" he said. "You can't float away again, Mr. Noah. You are safely tied up. Now do come ashore and tell us all your adventures!"

"Thank you!" said Mr. Noah, as he jumped down to the jetty. "It's lovely to sail away on the big wide sea—but it's much, MUCH nicer to come home again."

NODDY
and the
RUNAWAY WHEEL

Now one day when Noddy was coming back from Humming-Top Village, he heard a loud POP! His little car began to sway about, and Noddy stopped at once. What had happened?

"Oh dear—a puncture!" said Noddy, as he bent down to look at the wheel. "In my back wheel— what a nuisance. Thank goodness I've my spare wheel with me!"

Well, it wasn't long before Noddy took off the punctured wheel, to put his spare one in its place. He was so busy that he didn't see little Ben Bunny peeping at him . . .

He didn't see Ben standing the old wheel up,

and giving it a push. Oh dear — down the hill rolled the wheel, bumpity-bump! Now for a fine run!

Noddy finished putting on the spare wheel, and then looked round for the punctured one. It wasn't there!

"Where are you, wheel?" he said. "Where have you hidden yourself?"

Aha! Ben Bunny could tell you, Noddy.

The wheel is a long way away, with Ben running after it. It is bumping along at top speed, having a lovely time.

It met Big-Ears on his bicycle, and almost bumped into him, but Big-Ears JUST managed to ride
into a ditch. He fell off, bump! How cross he
was!

"That looks like one of Noddy's car-wheels!"
he said, staring after it.

"Oh, my goodness, it's going to run into the milkman's cart. Stop, wheel!"

On went the runaway wheel, and BANG! It went straight into the milkman's cart. Bottles flew up in the air, and milk spouted all over the place.

The milkman was very angry. "Come back!" he

yelled to the wheel bumping happily off.

"Look out—the Skittle family are coming along. Look out, wheel!"

Down go the Skittles as the wheel runs right into them—bump and roll, bump and roll! Sally Skittle is most surprised.

It didn't stop. It ran straight at the poor Wobbly-Man and over he went — but he didn't fall down. No, he wobbled to and fro and then stood up straight.

"What hit me?" he said, in surprise. "I've got quite a dent in my middle!"

He stared after the wheel and gave a shout.

"Look out, Mr. Plod—hey, look out!"

Mr. Plod was standing in the street, directing

the traffic. The wheel came bounding towards him, and bumped him right over. He was MOST surprised.

There was soon quite a crowd round poor Mr. Plod. Mrs. Tubby Bear helped him up.

"That's Noddy's car wheel," she said. "Little

rascal, letting it run away like this! I nearly got knocked over with it too! He must have sent it rolling down the hill.''

"And he knocked me, and my milk-cart right over!'' said the milkman, crossly.

"And us too!'' said the Skittles.

"And that wheel tried to bump me over!" said
the Wobbly-Man. "Look at the dent in my middle.
Hark, what's that—parp-parp!"

It was Noddy coming along, hooting, looking
for his runaway wheel. How surprised he was
when Mr. Plod took hold of him and lifted him

angrily from his car! "Noddy, how DARE you send one of your car wheels rolling down the hill?" said Mr. Plod, sternly. "It knocked heaps of people over, me as well. How DARE you do such a thing?"

"I didn't, didn't, didn't," said Noddy, in

surprise. "Oh, don't lock me up, Mr. Plod, please don't!"

But Mr. Plod marched him away, and the little car said "parp-parp" very sadly indeed.

Look at Noddy sitting all by himself in a tiny cell, feeling very sad. Outside he can hear his

little car hooting softly. It has run after him!

But who is this coming along through the village? It's Mrs. Bunny, with naughty little Ben Bunny!

"Please, where is Noddy?" she says. "Ben has done something very naughty!"

Mrs. Bunny saw Mr. Plod and went to him.

"Mr. Plod, my little Ben Bunny did a dreadful thing this morning—he rolled Noddy's car wheel down the hill! I hope it didn't knock anyone over, Mr. Plod."

The policeman frowned at Ben Bunny.

"So it wasn't Noddy!" he said. "It was you! And I've locked up poor little Noddy!"

Mr. Plod brought Noddy out, and pointed to Ben Bunny. "He rolled away your wheel!" he said. "Bend over, Ben Bunny. I'm going to give you a very good smacking!"

"No, no," said Noddy, "he's only a very little Bunny. Let him go!"

Mrs. Bunny was so glad. She took Noddy to the dairy and bought him an enormous ice-cream!

NODDY'S AEROPLANE

"There's Mrs. Tubby's brother," says Noddy. "He's going to land his aeroplane in my garden."

Airman Tubby jumps out. "Noddy, do be kind. Lend me your car to take Mrs. Tubby and Mrs. Noah for a picnic. They can't have a picnic up in the air."

"Yes, you can drive my car," nods Noddy. "You can fly my aeroplane," say Airman Tubby, "it's easy to fly. You don't have to bother about corners." Noddy only needs one lesson.

Then up in the air he goes, flying by himself. He is singing at the top of his voice!

"Oh, would you believe it, I've learnt to fly;
Up in the air I go, oh so high!
I might find a rainbow, a-glittering bright,
And bring it back—what a wonderful sight!"

But instead he finds Big-Ears' toadstool house. Down, down he goes, a
lands with a bump on the grass. "I'm so glad you came, Noddy," says Big-Ea
"I'm in a great hurry to catch the steamer."

and then whirr-rr-rrr-rrr! Noddy was away at top speed. "Be careful, Noddy!" shouts Big-Ears. "Bridges aren't made for flying under. I nearly lost my hat." But Noddy doesn't hear.

Look what the plane is doing now. "COME DOWN!" shouts Mr. Plod. Noddy swoops down—over goes a lamp-post!
"Sorry, sorry, sorry!" yells Noddy.

Big-Ears is very cross. "How dare you fly so low, Noddy!" he shouts. "I'm fat and heavy, and I don't want to land on someone's chimney. Now LET ME OUT! I'll go by train, it's *much* safer."

"I do so enjoy flying the aeroplane," Noddy thinks. "What shall I make it do next? Can it rock like the rocking horses? Oh, dear. It can." Doesn't it look funny?

Then Noddy sees the Clockwork Clowns all turning head-over-heels. That's NOT what aeroplanes are for, Noddy. Go up high, and fly properly!

"Hey—you're flying upside-down, Noddy," shout the Humming Tops. "You'll fall out."

But he slides back into his seat. Then he sees Big-Ears getting into the steamer.

Noddy lands and says "Won't you fly with me now?"
"I don't want to talk to you," says Big-Ears, "till you do something useful with that aeroplane."

Perhaps someone else would like to fly. Yes, a Sailor Doll wants to. "Take me to my soldier brother at the Toy Fort," he says.

This time Noddy flies carefully. They land quite gently right by the sailor doll's brother. "I'll tie the aeroplane to the sentry box while we're talking," says the sailor Doll.

The Captain of the Soldiers rushes up. "How dare you talk to a soldier when he'
on duty!" he roars. "Take that aeroplane away."
And he cuts the rope. Off flies the aeroplane.

Up, up into the sky flies Noddy, all on his own. "Oh dear, it's not easy to do anything useful with an aeroplane," he says sadly. He bumps into a little cloud. Then he bumps into a balloon.

"What are you doing up here, monkeys? And you too, kangaroos?" They have escaped from Mr. Noah's Ark.

Noddy ties the balloon to his aeroplane, and pulls the bad monkeys and kangaroo
back to the Ark. "Here you are, Mr. Noah; it's a good thing I had an aeroplane
today," he calls, "I couldn't have caught them in my little car."
Mr. Noah is pleased. "I shall tell Big-Ears how useful you have been," he says.

arp-parp-PARP! What's that? Why it's Noddy's car. Airman Tubby has ought Mrs. Noah back from the picnic in it. "Now you can stop flying, Noddy," e says. "I think it's safer if you drive your little car." Noddy thinks so too. e jumps into it and sings a very loud song.

"Oh here's my little car again,
I won't drive in a train or plane,
I'll drive *you*, funny little car!
You're jigging up and down for me,
Parp-parping as we go,
So everybody turns to see
And says 'Here comes Noddy, hallo!'"